W9-DAG-720
03/2019

PALM BEACH COUNTY
LIBRARY SYSTEM
3650 Summit Boulevard
West Palm Beach, FL 33406-4198

Dear Parents:

Congratulations! Your child is taking the first steps on an exciting journey. The destination? Independent reading!

STEP INTO READING® will help your child get there. The program offers five steps to reading success. Each step includes fun stories and colorful art or photographs. In addition to original fiction and books with favorite characters, there are Step into Reading Non-Fiction Readers, Phonics Readers and Boxed Sets, Sticker Readers, and Comic Readers—a complete literacy program with something to interest every child.

Learning to Read, Step by Step!

Ready to Read   Preschool–Kindergarten
• big type and easy words • rhyme and rhythm • picture clues
For children who know the alphabet and are eager to begin reading.

Reading with Help   Preschool–Grade 1
• basic vocabulary • short sentences • simple stories
For children who recognize familiar words and sound out new words with help.

Reading on Your Own   Grades 1–3
• engaging characters • easy-to-follow plots • popular topics
For children who are ready to read on their own.

Reading Paragraphs   Grades 2–3
• challenging vocabulary • short paragraphs • exciting stories
For newly independent readers who read simple sentences with confidence.

Ready for Chapters   Grades 2–4
• chapters • longer paragraphs • full-color art
For children who want to take the plunge into chapter books but still like colorful pictures.

STEP INTO READING® is designed to give every child a successful reading experience. The grade levels are only guides; children will progress through the steps at their own speed, developing confidence in their reading. The F&P Text Level on the back cover serves as another tool to help you choose the right book for your child.

Remember, a lifetime love of reading starts with a single step!

For Jeanne,
who grows a garden of friends!
—C.R.

To Laura and Paul,
for being the best bestest friends
—E.M.

Text copyright © 2019 by Candice Ransom
Cover art and interior illustrations copyright © 2019 by Erika Meza

All rights reserved. Published in the United States by Random House Children's Books, a division of Penguin Random House LLC, New York.

Step into Reading, Random House, and the Random House colophon are registered trademarks of Penguin Random House LLC.

Visit us on the Web!
StepIntoReading.com
rhcbooks.com

Educators and librarians, for a variety of teaching tools, visit us at RHTeachersLibrarians.com

Library of Congress Cataloging-in-Publication Data is available upon request.

ISBN 978-1-5247-2040-7 (trade) — ISBN 978-1-5247-2041-4 (lib. bdg.) — ISBN 978-1-5247-2042-1 (ebook)

Printed in the United States of America
10 9 8 7 6 5 4 3 2 1

This book has been officially leveled by using the F&P Text Level Gradient™ Leveling System.

Garden Day!

by Candice Ransom
illustrated by Erika Meza

Random House 🏠 New York

Bunnies hop.

Robins sing.

Time to plant!

Wake up, spring!

Grab the hoe,
bucket, rake.

Long black hose
looks like a snake!

This sunny spot
is good for seeds.

First we have to pull those weeds!

Pick up rocks.

Smash dirt clumps.

Mister Toad

shows off his jumps!

Dig small holes.

Use the hoe.

Let our peas have
room to grow.

Drop the seeds
into the row.

Push dirt over
with your toe.

Hungry crow
spots a treat.

17

Go find ants and
worms to eat!

These old pants,
this old shirt.

Make a scarecrow.

Stick in the dirt.

Working hard.

Hot sun. Phew!

Water garden—

and you, too!

Read our sign—

"Seeds in the ground."

28

Peas are growing.

Please step around.

Farm stand trip.

Popcorn to munch.

We eat carrots
by the bunch.

Buzzing bees.

Back yard swing.

See our garden!

Hello, spring!